With love to our little angel, Zach
~ Mimi

THE WISE ANIMAL HANDBOOK

Kate B. Jerome

ARCADIA KIDS

Attempt new skills from time to time.

Just try to think them through.

And if you find you're left behind...

...then change your point of view.

Try not to think of just yourself.

Invent new ways to share.

Stay close to friends whom you can trust.

But always be aware.

Avoid the tattle in the tale.

Insist that truth is best.

Embrace with pride the strengths you have.

Demand to be impressed.

Enjoy the peace that nature brings.

Ignore what's just for show.

Join forces when the road gets rough.

Admit when you don't know.

Remember family is the best.

Despite the ups and downs.

Don't hide from things that you must face.

Make joyful laughing sounds.

Eat healthy food to grow up strong.

Be patient with your friends.

Try not to take a stubborn stand.

Be quick to make amends.

Excuse yourself when manners slip.

Be helpful every day.

Keep trying even when it's hard.

But
don’t
forget to
play!

And sing

... and dance each day!

Written by Kate B. Jerome
Design and Production: Lumina Datamatics, Inc.
Coloring Illustrations: Tom Pounders
Research: Eric Nyquist

Cover Images: See back cover

Interior Images: 002 Anetapics/Shutterstock.com; 003 George Green/Shutterstock.com; 004 Sergey Uryadnikov/Shutterstock.com; 005 Gnomeandi/Shutterstock.com; 006 Bruce MacQueen/Shutterstock.com; 007 Henk Bentlage/Shutterstock.com; 008 M.M./Shutterstock.com; 009 Mikael Damkier/Shutterstock.com; 010 Brendan van Son/Shutterstock.com; 011 Michael Pettigrew/Shutterstock.com; 012 StevenRussellSmithPhotos/Shutterstock.com; 013 Pakhnyushchy/Shutterstock.com; 014 Patjo/Shutterstock.com; 015 Quinn Martin/Shutterstock.com; 016 Lincoln Rogers/Shutterstock.com; 017 Dirk Ercken/Shutterstock.com; 018 Karel Gallas/Shutterstock.com; 019 Orangecrush/Shutterstock.com; 020 Guenter-foto/Shutterstock.com; 021 Janecat/Shutterstock.com; 022 Shironina/Shutterstock.com; 023 Annette Shaff/Shutterstock.com; 024 Vitaly Titov/Shutterstock.com; 025 Rohappy/Shutterstock.com; 026 MattiaATH/Shutterstock.com; 027 Otsphoto/Shutterstock.com; 028 FikMik/Shutterstock.com; 029 Four Oaks/Shutterstock.com; 030 Ekaterina Kolomeets/Shutterstock.com; 031 Hugh Lansdown/Shutterstock.com.

Published by Arcadia Kids, a division of Arcadia Publishing and
The History Press, Charleston, SC

For all general information contact Arcadia Publishing at:
Telephone: 843-853-2070
Email: sales@arcadiapublishing.com

For Customer Service and Orders:
Toll Free: 1-888-313-2665
Visit us on the Internet at www.arcadiapublishing.com

Library of Congress Cataloging-in-Publication data is on file with the publisher.

Printed in China

New Jersey State Butterfly

Black Swallowtail

Read Together

The black swallowtail was named the state butterfly in 2016 and can be found in all 21 counties of the state.

New Jersey State **Bird**

Eastern Goldfinch

Read Together

The eastern goldfinch was named the state bird of New Jersey in 1935. This little bird builds nests all over the Garden State.

New Jersey State Bug

Honeybee

Read Together

The honeybee was made New Jersey's state bug in 1974. A group of schoolchildren from Sunnybrae Elementary School in Hamilton Township came up with the idea!

New Jersey State Fish

Brook Trout

Read Together

The brook trout was named the state fish in 1992. Since the brook trout is so sensitive to pollution, having them in local streams and rivers is a sign of great water quality.